For Joseph & Jeannette

THE HYENA WHO WOULDN'T LAUGH!

by
PARIS & TAYLOR™

During the *dry* season, Africa is a *dusty* bowl!

Everyone hangs out at their *favorite* water hole!

It's a place where they can *escape* the heat.

And it's a place where *new* friends can meet.

It's a *happy* area *everyone* happened to love.

Except for *someone* who watched from above!

A hyena named Harry lived in the crack of a tree.
The hyena *hated everyone* who he could see!

He watched the animals. *Anger* filled his eyes!
He *disliked* them all! From the rhinos to the flies!

He *hated* the zebra, the hippo, the lion and *even* the giraffe.

This hyena was the *worst* kind of all! He just *wouldn't* laugh!

"Can't they be *quiet* like me. I *never* have much to say!

I always keep to myself and I *like* it that way!

All they do is make noise!" Harry said with a frown.

"From the moment the sun rises, until it goes down!"

"Then, when nightfall comes, they leave and go home.

But the *next* morning they're back!" he said with a moan.

"I would do *anything* to bring that *awful* racket to a halt.

And I *wouldn't* feel guilty. Why should I? It's *their* fault!"

The hyena began pacing. He was *too* upset to sit.

He walked on his rug 'til he *wore* a hole through it!

"It's *so* noisy," he grumbled, "I *can't* hear myself think!

It's *all* because of that place where *they* come to drink!"

Then, he stopped. "Drink, that's it—*of course*!"
He exclaimed without the *tiniest* bit of remorse!

"If I *take* those *noisy* animals' water away,
They would *no* longer have a *reason* to stay!"
Then that old hyena, that *crafty* old man,
Thought of a *crafty* old water-stealing plan!

First he *snuck* past the animals' favorite place.
He crept by with some grass *hiding* his face!

Next, he had to find someone. He *knew* where to go.

He found that someone atop a low-lying plateau!

Sitting watching the *dusty* plains below,
Lived this creature, the *lowest* of the low!

He *wasn't* to be trusted! From his mouth dripped lie after lie!
This beast was the vulture king—the *undertaker* from the sky!

Harry said the water hole was giving him a fit.

Then he *whispered* how he was going to *solve* it!

The vulture listened closely and *liked* what he heard.

For the *first* time, a smile crossed the face of that bird!

"No problem," the bird said. "I'll help you.

I *love* your plan for making the others blue!"

"Without that water, they *won't* last long at all.

Once they *kick off*, we vultures will have a ball!

For we get by, living off others' *bad* fortunes.

We'll all have a feast with *extra* large portions!"

"Helping," he added, "*won't* be a problem, you see.

All I have to do is alert *every* member of my family!"

"I'll get help from my sister, my father, his aunt and her brother.

If her arthritis *isn't* acting up, we'll get help from my grandmother!"

He was at his *next* stop. His *cold* heart filled with glee.

He reached a forest lined with papyrus after papyrus tree!

Wasting no time, the hyena rolled up his sleeves

And began *robbing* the branches of their leaves!

Grunting, he gathered the leaves into a stack
And headed home with the papyrus on his back!

Soon he was back. The hyena's timing was just right.

The sun had set. He could work by the *cover* of night!

He *stepped* into the water. He *waded* up to his knees.

Then he began *dunking* the papyrus he *stole* from the trees!

The leaves *soaked* up the water, *robbing* the hole blind!
Soon the hyena was done. He left *only* one drop behind!

The hyena used *all* his strength. He *sweated* and *strained*!

Then he *dragged* the leaves away from the hole he drained!

He *clucked* and *barked*. He *dragged* the pile for most of the night.

He left it where the vultures would fly it off with the next day's light!

Harry *raced* back. He *wanted* to get there before sunrise.

He *wanted* to see the pit and the animals' look of surprise!

He was back. Seeing the animals *didn't* bother him a bit.

In fact, Harry *smiled* as he watched them stare at the pit!

They were *staring* at that drop Harry *accidentally* left.

"I thought," he said, "I committed the *perfect* theft!"

"Now," Harry said, "their *friendliness* will *stop*!
Soon they will be *fighting* over that *last* drop!"

Instead, she *gave* it to Harry, catching him by surprise.

All of the others *smiled* at the hyena with *kind* eyes.

Harry *couldn't* speak. His mouth made *only* one sound.

It was a *clanging* noise as it *dropped* and *hit* the ground!

Over that drop, he *couldn't* believe they *didn't* fuss!

Over that drop, he *couldn't* believe they *didn't* cuss!

"They *needed* it," he said. "*That* I could see.

Instead, of *all* animals, they gave it to *me*!"

"*Me*, who has *never* laughed or had *any* fun.

Me, who has *never* shown kindness to anyone."

Hanging his head in *shame* and *disbelief*,

He said, "They were *kind* to me—*a thief*!"

Harry's problem was *no one* had given him *anything* before.

By *getting* that drop, he was about to be *changed* forevermore!

Slowly, the years of anger *melted* away.

Harry became a *new* someone that day!

Being *new*, he *had* to do what was right.

So he brought his crime *into* the light.

He *admitted* he stole the water. He said *he* was the one.

Again the animals *forgave* him for what he had done!

He said he'd *get* the water. He knew *where* to go.

But just then he was *covered* by a *giant* shadow!

It came from up above in the morning sky,

Where *all* of the vultures were *thundering* by!

Their numbers *blocked* the sun and *turned* the sky black!

Harry *knew* what he had to do to get the water back!

He *ran* after the birds who were completing *his* crime!

Harry *hoped* he would be able to stop them in time!

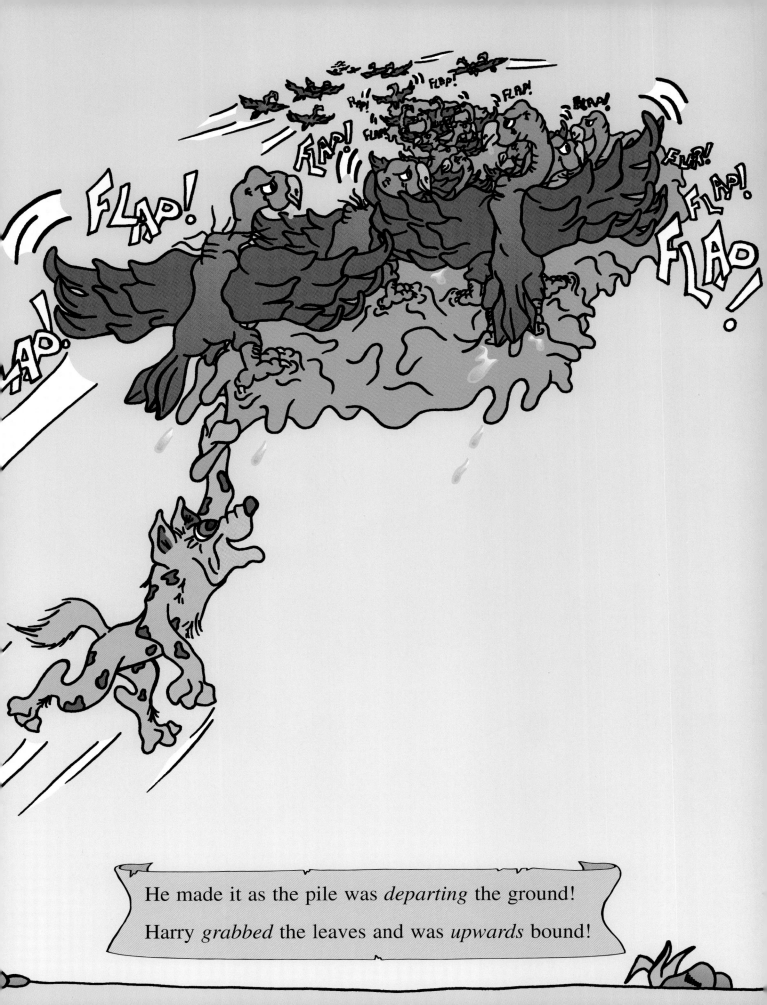

He made it as the pile was *departing* the ground!

Harry *grabbed* the leaves and was *upwards* bound!

The bird king saw our pal as the pile continued to climb.

"Harry," the vulture squawked, "you made it *just* in time!"

"No," Harry shouted, "I'm here to *end* your joy-ride!

For I've *changed* and become a *new* someone inside!"

Our pal *plucked* a feather from one bird's breast,

And began *tickling* the toes of all the rest.

The birds tried to hold the pile but they could not.

For Harry the Hyena had *found* their ticklish spot!

Harry's tickle tactic worked, just as he planned.

Both he and the leaves were *headed* towards the land!

The empty hole was the place where he happened to drop!

The fall *pushed* the water from the leaves, filling the hole to its top!

Harry *crawled* out of the pit. He *wasn't* hurt at all.

The *leaves* and the *muddy* hole *cushioned* his fall!

His body was *covered* with gunk. He was a *funny* sight.

The animals began to *laugh* at him with *all* of their might!

Harry *spotted* his reflection, and what's more,
He did *something* he'd *never* done before!

Harry *finally* laughed as he stood up nice and tall.

And he laughed at *himself* which is the *best* laugh of all!

All it took was some *kindness* to turn Harry around.

Today, the water hole's the *spot* where *he* can be found!

SPECIAL ANNOUNCEMENT!

THE BIRD WHO WAS AFRAID OF HEIGHTS!

BOOK # 15
Collect Them All!

by PARIS & TAYLOR™

This is my *little* friend Paully. His book is *absolutely* fantastic!

This book is GREAT!

CHECK LIST PAGE!
Check off the book you have!
Visit our web site at: www.parisandtaylor.com

You have my book! Now get the rest! They're Great!

THE WORLD'S GREATEST CHILDREN'S BOOKS!™

- [ ] THE ELEPHANT WHO COULDN'T REMEMBER!
- [ ] THE TURTLE WHO FELT BOXED IN!
- [ ] THE BIRD WHO DIDN'T WANT TO FLY SOUTH FOR THE WINTER!
- [ ] THE BIRD WHO WAS AFRAID TO CLEAN THE CROCODILE'S TEETH!
- [ ] THE BEAR WHO COULDN'T HIBERNATE! (SLEEP)
- [ ] THE STRAW THAT DIDN'T BREAK THE CAMEL'S BACK!
- [ ] THE SKUNK WHO DIDN'T WANT TO STINK!
- [ ] THE OPOSSUM WHO DIDN'T WANT TO PLAY DEAD ANYMORE!
- [ ] THE PENGUIN WHO HATED THE COLD BECAUSE HE WAS ALL DRESSED UP AND HAD NO PLACE TO GO!
- [ ] THE ROOSTER WHO DIDN'T WANT TO WAKE UP EARLY ANYMORE!
- [ ] THE PIG WHO DIDN'T WANT TO GET DIRTY!
- [ ] THE LEMMING WHO DIDN'T WANT TO TAKE THE PLUNGE!
- [ ] THE FISH WHO COULDN'T SWIM!
- [x] THE HYENA WHO WOULDN'T LAUGH!
- [ ] THE BIRD WHO WAS AFRAID OF HEIGHTS!
- [ ] THE EAGLE WHO DIDN'T WANT TO WEAR HIS GLASSES ANYMORE!
- [ ] AND MORE!